KT-365-550

THERE'S A
DRAGON
IN MY
TOILET!

TOM NICOLL

ILLUSTRATED BY
SARAH HORNE

Stripes

CHAPTER 1
PAN THE PARTY PLANNER

"Echo-Romeo-India-Charlie, I have eyes on the objective. The chickens are in the hen house. I repeat, the chickens are in the hen house."

I looked blankly at the walkie-talkie in my hand. We didn't have a hen house. Or chickens. I clicked the button to talk. "Pan, what are you on about?" I asked.

Even above the noise of all the people gathered behind me in my living room, I could hear Pan sighing on the other end. "It's code, Eric," he said. "Honestly, are

5

Mini-Dragons the only ones who know how to use walkie-talkies properly?"

"No, but not everyone gets to hang around the house all day learning stuff from old cop movies," I said.

"Fine. The message is: your parents are here," he said. "And now that I've finished being lookout, can I come downstairs?"

"In a couple of minutes," I said. "Come down once they're inside. I'll meet you in the hall and then you can hide in my pocket."

"Ah, the glamorous life of a Mini-Dragon," said Pan.

I turned to face the room. "All right, everyone, it's time," I shouted before switching off the lights.

There was silence, followed by the sound of the front door opening, footsteps walking through the hall, the opening of the door, the clicking of the light switch, then:

"SURPRISE!!"

"Arrrrrrrgggggghhhhhhh!!!" screamed
Mum.

"Arrrrrrrgggggghhhhhhh!!!" screamed
Dad.

"Mum, Dad, relax! It's OK!" I said.

"Eric?" said Mum, her fright turning to
confusion. "What is all this?"

I glanced back at the dozens of people
in our living room wearing party hats, the
balloons scattered everywhere, the brightly
coloured gift boxes piled in a corner and the
huge 'Happy Anniversary' banner draped
from the ceiling.

I thought it was kind of obvious.

"It's a surprise party," I said.

"Oh, right," said Mum, nodding slowly.
"For who?"

I slapped my forehead. "For you and Dad, of course. Happy twentieth wedding anniversary!"

"HAPPY ANNIVERSARY!" bellowed everyone behind me.

My parents stared at each other in shock.

"Well," said Dad. "It's certainly a surprise."

"You have Eric to thank for that," said my Auntie Ruth, appearing next to me. She had been looking after us while Mum and Dad were out. "Organized the whole thing himself."

My parents' heads turned sharply back towards me. They looked even more surprised than before.

"This was all you?" asked Dad, unable to hide the doubt in his voice.

He was right to be doubtful, of course. I hadn't organized this by myself. In fact, I'd hardly done any of it. I just happened to be good friends with a Mini-Dragon. And Mini-Dragons are excellent at party planning.

The whole idea had been Pan's to begin with. Once he'd found out that my parents' anniversary was coming up, he had been like a Mini-Dragon possessed. I think maybe he wanted to do something nice for them to try and make up for all the trouble he had caused since his arrival. Or maybe it was just because he had enjoyed my last birthday party so much. Now *that* was a good party, though hopefully this time we could avoid firing anyone into a tree in a rocket-powered scooter.

Pan's party planning had consisted of:

- Organizing the catering over the phone. I had a bit of a task convincing him to order anything other than prawn crackers though.

- Making all the decorations, although he struggled with the balloons — accidentally blowing fire into them instead of air.

- Drawing up the guest list, sending out invitations to all my parents' friends and family. We had to sneak a look in Mum's diary for their addresses.

- Engineering an elaborate plot where he phoned up Dad and pretended to be a radio-show host claiming that he had won a free meal at a top restaurant in town. That restaurant was Panda Cottage, the Chinese restaurant that had once delivered Pan to my house inside a box of beansprouts.

- Our friend Min was able to convince her parents, the owners of said restaurant, to cover the bill. This gave us plenty of time to get everything set up and also allowed Min to tip us off when my parents were leaving.

Of course I could hardly tell my parents that a Mini-Dragon had arranged their party, so I smiled and nodded, taking all the credit.

"But ... how did you afford everything?" said Mum, looking panicked. "Tell me you've not been using our credit cards?"

"I've not been using your credit cards," I said, rolling my eyes.

"Of course he hasn't, Maya," said Auntie Ruth. "We all chipped in."

"Oh," said Mum. "Well ... I don't know what to say. Thank you, Eric. This is lovely."

I could see her eyes beginning to well up and I knew what was coming next. She wrapped her arms around me, squeezing me to within an inch of my life, then planted a massive kiss on my face.

"Yeah, nice one, son," said Dad,

punching me affectionately on the arm.

Suddenly a flash of light almost blinded us.

"Pic-ture," said Posy, my two-and-a-half-year-old sister, wielding her new favourite toy – a kid's camera that my auntie Ruth had bought her.

She was obsessed with it, always popping up when you least expected it to take a photo. It was a bit of a nuisance, especially as I had to check it all the time in case she snapped Pan. Usually it was OK because Mini-Dragons can freeze themselves if they sense danger so mostly he just looked like a toy. But she was sneakier than you'd expect a toddler to be and the camera also had a video mode, so I couldn't take any chances. On this occasion however I was only too happy to pose for Posy. She took one of me, Mum and Dad, and then Auntie Ruth took one of the four of us.

Pictures out of the way, I left my parents to mingle with the rest of our friends and family. The Blooms, our next-door neighbours, had turned up, too. Mr Bloom was like a bigger version of his son Toby – the same curly hair, the same bright red cheeks and the same appetite. Together they had taken the buffet table hostage, the pair of them busy stuffing their faces with prawn crackers (well, I had to let Pan order *some*, didn't I?). Mrs Bloom stood next to them dressed in something my mum called a 'Power Suit', which isn't nearly as exciting as it sounds. Unlike her family, Mrs Bloom showed no interest in the buffet, or anything else for that matter other than the phone she was tapping away on.

"Mini-Dragons sure know how to throw a party," said Jayden, appearing at my side, with Min.

"Yeah ... they ... sure ... do," she panted. "Sorry ... cycled ... over ... here ... as quickly ... as I ... could ... after your ... parents left. Where is ... Pan, anyway?"

"Surely you let him come?" said Jayden. "After he put in so much work?"

"Of course," I said. "As if I could stop him even if I wanted to. He was going to come down and hide in my pocket once my parents arrived. I'll go and get him."

I walked out to the hall, where we'd arranged to meet, but there was no sign of Pan.

"That's weird," I said, stepping back into the living room. "He's not there."

"Give him a shout," suggested Jayden, pointing towards my walkie-talkie.

"Right, yeah," I said, clicking the call button. "Pan. Are you coming? Pan?"

There was no reply.

The three of us looked at each other with the same anxious expression on our faces. I could tell we were all thinking the same thing. Pan wasn't the type of Mini-Dragon to take his time joining a party. To be honest, I don't know if there *is* a type of Mini-Dragon who does like to take their time, but Pan definitely isn't one of them.

It was time to start worrying.

"Where could he be?" asked Min.

I already knew the answer to that. Whenever Pan went missing, the same person was always involved.

"Where is he?" I said, storming up to Toby.

"Mmph?" said Toby, a sausage roll

sticking out of his mouth.

"Eric!" bellowed Toby's dad. "Good to see you, lad. Always a pleasure to see Toby's best pal. Isn't that right, Margery?"

Mrs Bloom's eyes flickered from her phone screen to me for a second before she resumed her tapping.

"He's not my best pal," said Toby, visibly insulted by the idea. "Eric's like my nemesis."

Mr Bloom laughed. "Ha. Listen to him, Eric. Nemesis, my foot! He's always going on about you. Tells us whenever you get something new and begs us to buy him the same thing. Between you and me, I think he looks up to you."

"Gah! Shut up!" snapped Toby, his face bright red. Before his dad could speak again, Toby grabbed a tray of sausage rolls with one hand and me with the other and led me across the room.

"What do you want?" he asked, stuffing another sausage roll into his mouth.

"Now, Toby," I said. "That's no way to talk to your hero, is it?"

Toby shot me a fierce look. "Very funny, Crispo," he said.

"The Mini-Dragon," I said. "Where is he?"

Toby removed the sausage roll. "What, you mean the toy you never let me borrow even though I always promise to bring it back? How should I know?"

"Because whenever he goes missing, you're the one behind it," I said. I could feel the anger rising in my face.

"*He?*" said Toby. "I know it's realistic, with its talking and flame-farting, but you're talking about this toy like it's real. You're losing it, Crispo."

"Come on, Eric, let's go," said Min as she and Jayden came over and pulled me away.

"But he's got—" I began.

"I don't think he does," said Jayden. "Toby's a rubbish liar. I think he's telling the truth."

"Hey!" protested Toby. "I'm a great liar, actually. Maybe I really do have your stupid toy."

I looked at Toby carefully for a moment then turned to Jayden. "Yeah, you're right, he doesn't have him."

"Yes, I do!" said Toby as we walked away.

"Where can he be, then?" I asked, ignoring Toby.

"Let's split up," said Min. "I'll check out in the street. Jayden, you look around the party, make sure he hasn't decided to mingle with the guests. Eric, you search the rest of the house."

I nodded, then left the others and went to check the kitchen first.

No luck. I was about to head upstairs when Pusskin, our over-sized, over-pampered, over-evil cat wandered past me.

"Pusskin," I said suspiciously. "You haven't seen Pan, have you?"

Being a cat, Pusskin didn't reply. Instead

she looked at me with total disdain, stuck her nose in the air and wandered off to the kitchen. I knew Pusskin hated Pan – and had once tried to eat him – but ever since almost having her whiskers burnt off, she seemed to have lost interest.

Just to be sure though, I quickly checked the cupboard under the stairs where Pan sometimes hid from her. Nothing.

I was starting to panic. I mean, it wasn't like we could just put up a Missing Poster:

MISSING

HAVE YOU SEEN THIS MINI-DRAGON?

REWARD: £3.57 (sorry, it's all I have left from my pocket money)

DESCRIPTION: Approximately 15cm tall, scaly

COLOUR: Green

EYES: Black

WINGS: Two

CLAWS: Sharp

TEETH: See "Claws"

EATS: prawn crackers, mountain goats, dirty washing

I opened my bedroom door and breathed a sigh of relief – Pan was curled up on my bed. But his walkie-talkie was lying on the floor and he looked miserable.

"Pan ... are you all right?" I asked.

He looked up, as if he hadn't heard me come in. "Hi, Eric," he said quietly. "Yeah, I'm OK, just feeling a bit run-down, that's all. I was on the way downstairs when I saw your parents and the rest of your family and suddenly ... I don't know, I felt a bit funny. Think I just need a good sleep."

"Oh," I said. "You're not coming to the party, then."

"No," he said, closing his eyes. "Think I'll give it a miss, if it's all the same to you."

"Of course," I said. "Hope you feel better soon."

"I'm sure I wi—" said Pan, his voice trailing off as he fell asleep. I took out the

small facecloth that Pan had been using as a
blanket from my sock drawer and placed it
over him.

I quietly left the room, meeting Min and Jayden on the landing.

"You found him?" asked Min.

I nodded.

"Is he all right?" asked Jayden, looking concerned.

"Yeah," I said. "I think he's just a bit tired from organizing everything. He'll be fine in the morning."

That's what I was trying to convince myself, anyway.

CHAPTER 2
CRACKING THE DRAGON CODE

It was two days later, the first Monday of the school holidays, and Min, Jayden and I were back in my room, watching Pan. He was lying on my bed again, staring at the wall, the gloomiest expression filling his tiny dragon face.

Jayden waved his hand in front of Pan. No reaction.

"What's wrong with him?" whispered Min.

"I don't know," I said. "He's been like this since the party. He sleeps in his drawer all night then spends all day on my bed. Sometimes he sleeps, but mostly he just lies there. Hardly says a thing."

"He looks like you've told him he has to go and live with Toby," said Jayden.

"He's not even touched his food," noted Min, pointing at the two unopened bags of prawn crackers beside him.

Pan let out a yawn.

"Is he ill?" asked Jayden.

"I'm not sure," I said. "Maybe."

"Have you consulted the *Encyclopaedia Dragonica*?" asked Min.

I jumped up. "Min, you're a genius," I said.

Min shrugged. "Yeah, I get that a lot."

The *Encyclopaedia Dragonica* is the ultimate guide to all things dragon. It's full of amazing facts like:

Encyclopaedia Dragonica

- Dragons only come in six different colours: red, green, black, white, gold and beige.

- Dragons are often thought to have majestic names like Zahira, Dracara or Faaaarrraaa the Magnificent. But actually, one of the most common dragon names is Steve.

- No dragon has *ever* captured a princess and forced her to live in a tower. These stories were made up by scheming knights in the Middle Ages who were hoping to marry royalty.

- Contrary to popular belief, dragons are not particularly interested in gold. They don't buy that much, and when they do they generally prefer to trade items or use credit cards.

Pulling the huge book out from under my bed, I began flicking through the pages.

"*Dragon illnesses, ailments and diseases,*" I said. "OK, let's see. What are his symptoms?"

Min put her hand on Pan's head. "He feels a bit warm," she said.

"I think that's normal," I said. "He does breathe fire after all."

"He's looking a bit green," noted Jayden.

"He's a green dragon," I said, rolling my eyes.

"More green, I mean," said Jayden. "Don't you think?"

"I'm not sure," I said, "but he's definitely tired and leff … leff… That thing where he moves like he's half asleep."

"Lethargic?" Min suggested.

"Yes, that's it," I said. "There must be something in here about lethargic dragons. Ah, here we go."

Encyclopaedia Dragonica

Dragons are solitary creatures. Spending too much time in the company of other dragons can exhaust them. They become lethargic, irritable and generally unpleasant to be around. Most dragons go their whole life without making friends and limit their family contact to birthdays and Christmas, when they generally put little effort into gift ideas.

The exception to this is Mini-Dragons. Mini-Dragons are the most sociable of all the dragons, and family and friendship are the most important things in the world to them. While a dragon tires easily from too much companionship, Mini-Dragons tire from too little.

Jayden, Min and I looked at each other.

"Well, it can't be that," said Jayden. "Pan has plenty of companionship. He's got us, hasn't he? How much more companionship does he need?"

Min rolled her eyes. "Don't you get it?" she said. "*Family* and friendship."

"He's homesick," I said, lifting Pan up and placing him gently on my knee. "Is that it, Pan?"

My Mini-Dragon remained silent.

"Pan," I said.

"Pan," I said again.

"Pan."

"Pan."

"Pan."

"Pan."

"What?" said Pan at last.

"Pan," I said gently, relieved to hear him speak. "We're just wondering if the reason you're a bit sad is because you're homesick?"

Pan shook his head. "No way," he said

in a dull voice. "Mini-Dragons are excellent at not being homesick."

"It would make sense if you were," I said. Pan's family lived in the mountains in China and he hadn't seen them for months. "Maybe seeing my family at the party made you realize how much you miss your mum and dad."

Pan seemed to think this over. "Perhaps a little," he admitted.

"Don't your parents have any way of contacting you?" asked Min.

"Well, yeah, but through my aunt and uncle," said Pan. "Only adult Mini-Dragons know how to use dragon codes."

Me, Jayden and Min looked blankly at each other.

"Dragon codes?" I asked.

Pan nodded. "Every Mini-Dragon family has one. It's a way for Mini-Dragons all over the world to communicate with each other. Each code is unique, but they all follow the same pattern – two parts separated by a curled-up Mini-Dragon."

"Do you know yours?" asked Jayden.

"Yes," said Pan. "I've seen it a few times. But it's not much use to me because, like I said, only adult Mini-Dragons know how to decipher them."

I reached for a notepad and the smallest pencil to hand. "Pan, do you think you could draw your dragon code for us anyway?"

Pan took the pencil from me, grasping it with both hands. It looked massive sandwiched between his two claws, and he struggled just to draw a straight line. Eventually he gave up, tossing the pencil away. He picked up the piece of paper, took a breath, then blew out a small blast of fire. The three of us jumped back in fright.

Pan held up the paper. Scorched on to it
was the following:

THELONGS_83@DRAGONNET.CN

Min, Jayden and I stared at the page for what seemed like ages, our mouths hanging open.

"I told you," said Pan. "It's gibberish."

Jayden raised his eyebrows. "Who wants to tell him?" he said.

CHAPTER 3
DEAR MUM AND DAD...

"Pan, that's an email address," I said.

"A what?" asked Pan.

Min put her hands over her eyes. "I don't get it," she said. "How can someone who knows so much possibly not know what an email address is?"

"It's not *that* unusual," said Jayden. "My parents are exactly the same."

"An email address, Pan," I said. "You use it to send messages to people over the internet. The Longs ... that's your family surname."

Pan looked confused. "But ... the dragon codes are ancient."

"He's right – no one uses email any more," said Min with a chuckle.

"But Dad used to go on a two-day trek to the nearest city to find a temple where he could use the dragon code," said Pan. "He always said that one day, when I was older, he would bring me along."

"Maybe by 'temple' he meant 'internet café'," suggested Jayden.

"Look, there's one way to find out if it's a real address," I said. "Let's email it."

Pan let out a little gasp. "Use the dragon code? But you're a ... human!"

Shaking my head, I stood up and opened my bedroom door. "Mum!" I shouted. "Is it OK if we use the computer?"

"That's fine, Eric," Mum shouted back. "But I'll need it in half an hour for my class."

Mum had been teaching yoga for years, but recently she had hit upon the idea of teaching classes online, live-streaming them to the entire world. She was making a fortune. I had even got a little boost in my pocket money for helping her set it up.

We went through to the computer room, which is what I call our spare room. My dad calls it Command Central, because it's the room he uses to plot his tactics for the Kippers. Mum calls it the yoga room because... Well, you can probably guess why. And if she could talk, Pusskin would probably call it *her* room, since it was where she spent most of her time. She was curled up in the desk chair, but as soon as she saw Pan she was out of the room in a shot.

"Bye, Pusskin," said Pan, smiling for the first time in ages.

I raised the lid of the laptop computer,

then clicked on the envelope icon. I logged into my email account and began typing:

SEND	SAVE	DISCARD

FROM: Eric Crisp

TO: THELONGS_83@DRAGONNET.CN

SUBJECT: Pan

I have your son. Please reply for more information.

"What?" I said, noticing that the others were giving me funny looks.

"It reads like a ransom note," said Min.

"You write it, then," I said, frowning.

"Fine, I will," said Min, shoving me out

of the way. She deleted what I had written
before cracking her knuckles and launching
into her own email.

| SEND | SAVE | DISCARD |

FROM: Eric Crisp

TO: THELONGS_83@DRAGONNET.CN

SUBJECT: Pan

Dear Mr and Mrs Long,
Hello! My name is Min, I'm a friend of your
son, Pan. I've heard so much about you both.
Pan told us all about those horrible people
knocking down your cave. Ridiculous! If I'd
been around, I'd have given them a piece
of my mind. Actually, I'd love to come over
there. I'm Chinese, too, you see, although
I was born in England. Next time I'm over
visiting relatives we should definitely meet
up. We could have lunch.

"Min!" I said. "Get to the point!"

"Yeah," said Jayden. "You're writing an email, not a book."

Min folded her arms. "I suppose you think you can do better?" she said.

"As a matter of fact I do," said Jayden.

SEND	SAVE	DISCARD

FROM: Eric Crisp

TO: THELONGS_83@DRAGONNET.CN

SUBJECT: Pan

Hi Mr and Mrs Long!
Have you seen this video of dogs playing snooker?
www.funnydogvids.com/snookerdogs

"Jayden!" I said.

"*What?*" protested Jayden. "It's an

icebreaker, isn't it? It's a *really* funny video."

As the three of us argued about what to put in the email, Pan jumped up on to the keyboard and began dancing across the keys, typing out his own message.

| SEND | SAVE | DISCARD |

FROM: Eric Crisp

TO: THELONGS_83@DRAGONNET.CN

SUBJECT: Pan

Raaaaarr raaaaarrrr rrrrrraaaaaaarrrr rrrar rrar rrrraaaaaaaaaaaaaarrr rarrr rrrrrraaaaarrrrr

There was an awkward silence as the three of us watched him type.

"Pan," I said softly. "I don't know how to put this…"

"Your email's gibberish," said Min bluntly.

"No, it isn't," said Pan. "Mini-Dragons have our own language."

"Oh," I said. Pan hadn't mentioned this before. He had taught himself how to speak English before we had even met so it had never been an issue. "What does your message say?"

"I just said it was me and that I was safe," said Pan. "And I asked them to reply."

He clicked the send button and the message vanished.

"Well … that's that, then," I said.

"Now what?" asked Jayden.

"Now we wait," said Min.

"I still don't think this is going to work," said Pan. "I'm telling you – only *adult* Mini-Dragons know the secrets of dragon codes. We're just wasting our—"

PING.

The four of us looked at the monitor. A little mail icon was flashing in the bottom corner of the screen.

"What's that?" asked Pan.

"It's a reply," I said, clicking on the icon. A message opened up on screen.

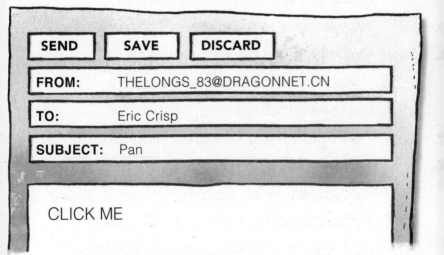

| SEND | SAVE | DISCARD |

FROM: THELONGS_83@DRAGONNET.CN

TO: Eric Crisp

SUBJECT: Pan

CLICK ME

"*Click me*?" I said.

"What does that mean?" asked Jayden.

"If I had to guess," said Min, "I think it means we should click on the link."

"Well, obviously," said Jayden. "What I mean is, you don't just click on random links in emails, do you? What if you opened a virus? It could wipe all the programs on your computer or steal all your information."

"Jayden's right," I said. "Mum would kill me if I downloaded a virus. I think we should take some time and think about this carefully."

Pan clicked on the link.

I sighed. "Or we could just do that."

A rotating egg timer appeared on screen. Moments later, a light beamed out of the webcam and then the four of us were staring back at ourselves from a little box in the corner of the screen. Then the egg timer vanished and in its place was a bigger box. Inside it were two Mini-Dragons.

"RAAAAAAAAARRRRRR!" they cried.

"MUM! DAD!" cried Pan.

CHAPTER 4
CATCHING UP

"I'm so happy to see you guys," said Pan.
"Oh ... I mean ... RARARRARRAAA."

The two Mini-Dragons looked at Pan
with surprise. "You speak English?" said
his mum. I could tell she was Pan's mum
because of:

a) Her high-pitched voice

b) Her long eyelashes

c) Her sparkling red claw-manicure

d) Her lack of a beard

Pan's dad had a wispy white beard that was almost as big as him. He also wore a pair of tiny metal-framed spectacles that made him look like a Mini-Dragon professor. "He's always been a clever boy, we should have known he would have picked up a language or two by now," he said, his face beaming with pride. Pan's parents both had the same hint of a Chinese accent that he did.

"I didn't know *you* spoke English," said Pan.

"Of course," said his mum, smiling fondly. "Your father and I learned to speak English when we went backpacking around Europe before you were born. Those were fun times. Oh, Pan, we were worried sick when your aunt and uncle told us you hadn't turned up in Mexico. We thought we might never—" She broke off mid-sentence as her eyes met mine for the first time. They flashed wild with fright before she let out an ear-piercing shriek.

"Pan! Behind you! Humans! **RUN!**" shouted Pan's dad.

"You touch my boy, so help me I'll find you and hunt you down," roared Pan's mum, shaking her little fists at the screen.

"I'm warning you, we have a very particular set of skills," warned her husband.

"They involve lots of fire!"

"Mum, Dad, it's OK," said Pan. "These are my friends."

There was a brief moment of silence.

"Sorry, son," said his father. "There must be a problem with the connection. It sounded like you said these humans were your *friends*."

"That's right," said Pan. "It's a long story."

"It would have to be," said his mum. "Well, let's hear it."

Of course they already knew how the story began – their family cave getting destroyed by builders. Pan's parents had planned to fly to the top of the mountains and settle there instead. But Pan hadn't got the hang of flying yet – to put it politely – so his parents had decided to send him to live with his aunt and uncle, bundling him into a container of beansprouts on a ship bound for Mexico.

Now Pan filled them in on what had happened next, starting with the detour the boxes made when the restaurant that had ordered them went out of business. Then his arrival in England at Min's parents' Chinese restaurant, Panda Cottage, and finally Min herself delivering Pan to our house in a takeaway on that fateful Friday night.

Pan's mum let out little gasps at each part of the story. Pan wisely avoided mentioning the two occasions he'd been dragon-napped by Toby.

"Oh dear," said Pan's dad, looking a little upset.

"It hadn't crossed my mind that the beansprouts would have ended up somewhere else."

"It's not your fault," said Pan. "You weren't to know that Panda Cottage Mexico would give food poisoning to a bunch of pro-wrestlers, forcing the owner to flee the country."

"I suppose that would be quite difficult to predict," agreed Mr Long.

"So these humans ... they're your ... friends?" asked Mrs Long, smiling nervously.

Pan nodded enthusiastically.

"Wonderful," she replied, in a voice that suggested she thought this was anything but. "What are their names?"

"This is Min and Jayden," said Pan.

"Nice to meet you," my friends chorused.

Pan's parents nodded and smiled politely.

"And this is Eric," said Pan, pointing

proudly at me. "He's been letting me sleep
in his sock drawer.

"His sock drawer?" said Pan's mum,
looking aghast.

Feeling a bit awkward, I smiled and gave
her a little wave.

"Don't be like that, Mum," said Pan. "It's
the best bed I've ever had. Much comfier
than sleeping on rocks like at home."

Her face softened a little. "Yes, well, I
suppose we must thank you, Eric, for looking
after our son," she said. "I hope he hasn't
been any trouble."

I stared at the screen, trying to figure
out how to answer that, then looked down
at Pan, who was waving his hands and
shaking his head furiously.

"Um..."

"Er..."

"Well..."

"No," I said, eventually. "No trouble at all."

"Well, I'm Mr Long," said Pan's dad. "But you can call me Cheng. And this is my wife Isabel—"

"And you can call me Mrs Long," she said firmly, before turning her attention back to Pan. "You look healthy enough. That's something, I suppose. How is the mountain goat in England anyhow? I've heard it's very bland over there."

Pan and I exchanged glances. "Actually, Mum, I haven't had that much goat recently. In fact, none at all."

Mrs Long looked horrified. "But you're a Mini-Dragon," she said. "What else could you possibly be eating?"

"They have these things called prawn crackers," said Pan.

"Prawn crackers?" she repeated, covering

her mouth. "Jumping dragons, it's worse than I thought."

"Oh, I don't know," said Pan's dad, "I used to quite enjoy a good prawn cracker. They are one of the three Mini-Dragon food groups, after all."

His wife shot him a look. "Yes, and so is dirty washing, if you believe everything you read. Would you have our son eating that, too?"

Pan's dad started to lick his snout. "Actually, I was always partial to a nice tea-stained vest as a boy. Or a good pair of muddy trousers. I was even known to enjoy a tomato-juice-soaked jumper from time to time. Had to be in the mood for those, mind you…"

"A growing Mini-Dragon should be eating mountain goat!" declared Pan's mum conclusively.

An awkward silence fell over the room. Min, Jayden and I stared at our shoes.

"Er … Mum, you look in great shape by the way," said Pan.

His mother smiled and waved him away. "Oh stop," she said.

"No, seriously," said Pan. "Have you been working out?"

"Well … yes, I have," she said proudly. "There are these yoga classes I've been watching on the internet. It's the only thing that's helped with the stress I've been under since you went missing. The woman that does it is a bit … *different* for my tastes, but she's a very good teacher. In fact, I'll have to go soon, her class starts in a few minutes."

The four of us looked at each other with stunned expressions. *Nah*, I thought, *it couldn't be… Could it?*

"What's wrong?" asked Mrs Long.

"Never mind," said Pan, squinting at the screen. I wondered what he was looking at, as all I could see in the background was a pile of rocks. "Wait … are you guys in the mountains right now?" asked Pan. "How can you be on the internet?"

"It's our new neighbours," replied his father excitedly. "Say what you want about them, and believe me, your mother did, but the humans that knocked down our old cave and put up all those new buildings sure know a thing or two about Wi-Fi. We even get a strong signal all the way up here in our new cave. With the Mini-Generator and laptop computer I picked up it means we don't have to keep going back and forth to internet cafés in the dead of night."

"Hang on … you 'picked up' a Mini-Generator and a laptop? You just went into a shop and bought them?"

His parents burst out laughing. "Oh, darling," said his mum. "Don't be so silly."

The little Mini-Dragon frowned. "So you stole them, then?"

The smiles on his parents' faces turned to shocked expressions. "Now, son," said Pan's dad, "how could you suggest such a thing? I admit, we didn't exactly walk up to the till, but we made sure the owners received fair payment."

Pan let out a groan. "You left them a goat, didn't you?"

"A *delicious* goat," corrected Pan's dad.

Pan shook his head in disbelief.

"Anyway, we must be going now," said his mum. "Yoga calls."

Pan looked a little sad. "Can we speak again soon?" he asked.

"Of course, sweetheart," she replied. "We'll have plenty of time to catch up

before Aunt Maria and Uncle Fernando
arrive at Eric's house."

"Oh, that's good," said Pan.

A pause.

"Wait... *What?*" said Pan. "Why are
they coming here?"

"We're sending them to get you, of course," she said. "Pan, we've been so worried – we've sent messages to all the Mini-Dragon families across the world. We've had Mini-Dragons searching the continents for you. Your dad and I must have flown across most of China ourselves. And your aunt and uncle have travelled all the way to Spain looking for you."

Mr Long made a little coughing noise. "Actually dear, they're on holiday," he said.

Mrs Long glared at her husband. "What? But they told me they had a tip— Oh, I should have known. Well, I suppose it doesn't matter now, I'll get them to pick you up on their way back to Mexico. Just let them even try getting out of it after lying to me."

Pan's face dropped. He looked even sadder than before. And this time I felt it, too – we all did. "But I don't want to live with them," he said. "They're horrible. I like it here, with Eric."

"Come on now, Pan," said Mrs Long in a soft voice. "I'm sure you've had an exciting time with your new … *friends*, and we're extremely grateful to them for looking after you, but your place is with your family. With other Mini-Dragons."

"But Mum—" protested Pan.

"Butting's for goats," said his father. "Now be a good boy and email us Eric's home address. Speak to you soon."

And with that, they were gone.

"Eric," shouted Mum from downstairs. "Wrap it up."

"OK," I shouted, my voice breaking as I spoke.

The four of us returned to my room. We sat down on my bed, and no one spoke for a long time.

CHAPTER 5
WAITING

We spent ages trying to come up with ways
to stop Pan having to leave. Here was what
we had:

1. Trick Pan's aunt and uncle into
   taking Toby to Mexico instead of
   Pan. Not sure how this would work —
   dress Toby up in a dragon costume
   perhaps? They might wonder about
   his weight though — too many prawn
   crackers?

2. Run away? I didn't think my mum would agree to this. Min pointed out that we wouldn't actually be asking for permission. Then Pan asked how we would get all the stuff out of my room. Min just shook her head and told us to forget it.

3. Move Pan to Min or Jayden's house for a while. Neither Min or Jayden seemed that keen on this even though I told them he's only actually destroyed my room once.

4. Send Pan to live with Toby — HAHAHA! No, come on, let's be serious here.

5. Convince Pan's parents to let him stay.

Number 5 seemed like our best shot, but the more Pan spoke to his parents, the better the Toby-in-a-dragon-costume idea seemed to get.

A few days later, Pan was in the computer room, speaking to his parents again. Min, Jayden and I were watching, hoping that he could talk them into changing their minds.

"I'm sorry, Pan, but the answer is no," said Pan's mum. "A Mini-Dragon's place is with other dragons."

"But why those Mini-Dragons?" asked Pan. "They're bullies."

Mr Long gave a little chuckle. "They're not bullies, they're ... well, they're..." He turned to his wife. "Help me out, Isabel."

"They're ... a bit stricter than we are," she agreed. "But that's not such a bad thing."

"Can't I at least come back home?" asked Pan.

"We've talked about this, son," said Mr Long. "Our altitude is too dangerous for a Mini-Dragon that can't fly."

"Well, why don't you guys come and live here?" suggested Pan. "There's plenty of room."

"Umm … Pan … hang on a second…" I started, before Pan's mum interrupted.

"The Longs have lived in these mountains for thousands of years," she said. "It's our home."

"It was my home, too," whispered Pan, hanging his head.

Pan's mum nodded. "Yes, and once your aunt and uncle finish your teaching, you can come back to it. I've spoken to them and they should be with you soon, so you might want to stop wasting the time you have left with your friends by arguing with us."

Once the call ended the four of us slunk back to my room, defeated.

"I don't want to go," said Pan. "All I wanted was to see my parents again, but now I'm going to lose my friends."

Min picked him up and gave him a kiss on the snout. "You'll always be our friend, Pan."

"Yeah," said Jayden. "We'll talk all the time online – now that you know what an email address is I'm sure we can get you into instant messaging, too."

The thought of being parted from Pan was unbearable, but I didn't want to think about it any more. "Your mum's right," I said, "about making the most of our time together. Let's do something other than moping about."

"Like what?" asked Pan, jumping out of Min's hand.

"We could play some games?" suggested Jayden.

Pan shook his head. "Not in the mood."

"Why don't we go out?" said Min.

"Nah," said Pan.

"We need to do *something*, Pan," I said. "Who knows how much time we have left. Do you really want to spend it sitting here waiting for your aunt and uncle to show up?"

Pan looked up at me defiantly. "No," he said. "You're right – let's go out. Bramble Park. I can ride the ducks again. Not the swans though, they didn't seem to like it last time."

"Yeah!" I said, punching the air. "Let's go! Wait – what's wrong?"

Pan's face had gone a bit red. "Nothing. Just realized I need to use the little dragon's room. Back in a minute."

We waited as Pan headed off to the

bathroom. About a minute later, I heard his tiny voice yell, "Eric, I think you'd better get in here."

I screwed up my face. "No, thanks!"

"Seriously, Eric, come here. Right now!"

I gave Min and Jayden a worried look and entered the bathroom, scared of what I might find. But all I saw was Pan standing on the edge of the toilet bowl, peering in.

"What is it?" I asked.

"Look," said Pan, pointing towards the water. Finally I could see what he was talking about. The water inside the toilet was bubbling. Little bubbles at first, but then bigger and bigger until—

WWHHHOOOOOSSSHHH!

A jet of water exploded out of the toilet, sending us both flying backwards.

And then there they were, walking towards us across the soaked bathroom floor. Two Mini-Dragons. Two miserable-looking Mini-Dragons in wetsuits, wearing little glass helmets on their heads.

They unzipped themselves then tossed aside their diving equipment.

It was fairly obvious which one was which – Aunt Maria was the taller of the pair by a couple of centimetres. She quickly wrapped her head in an expensive-looking silk scarf before putting on a pair of dark glasses, both of which she pulled from a small plastic bag. Uncle Fernando, meanwhile, was the roundest looking Mini-Dragon I had seen so far. The only thing he wore was a grumpy expression and a brown waterproof backpack.

Pan and I looked at each other. Bramble Park would have to wait.

CHAPTER 6
HELLO, GOODBYE

"So you're Erica, then?" said Uncle Fernando, a trace of a Spanish accent in his voice. "They said we should speak English, since you haven't bothered to learn Mini-Dragon."

"Eric," I said. "Erica is a girl's name."

Uncle Fernando looked at me suspiciously. "You're a boy, are you?" he asked.

"Yes," I said, annoyed by his rudeness. In fact I got the feeling he knew all this, but was just trying to wind me up for some reason.

The dumpy little dragon gave a shrug.
"You humans all look the same to me."

"What's going on?" asked Min, as she
and Jayden entered the bathroom behind us.

"Ugh, there's more of them," snapped Aunt Maria. "Pan Long, get away from those filthy humans right now. You don't know where they've been."

"*We're* filthy?" I said. "You two just came out of the toilet!"

"Of course we did," said Uncle Fernando. "Across the seas, it's a straight flight, but in the cities, the sewer network is the most efficient and safest way for a Mini-Dragon to travel. Every Mini-Dragon knows that."

"Pan, come here and give your aunt a kiss," said Aunt Maria.

A reluctant Pan had only taken a couple of steps towards her when she dragon-handled him into a hug and planted a smacker right on his snout. Under normal circumstances I might have had a good laugh, but somehow it didn't seem very funny right then.

"Let me get a good look at you," she

said, shoving Pan back. "Just as I thought – you're skin and bones. You don't look any bigger than when we saw you last year."

"That's because this human's had him living off prawn crackers," said Uncle Fernando.

"Actually, according to the *Encyclopaedia Dragonica*, prawn crackers contain everything a Mini-Dragon needs for a healthy diet," I said. If anything, I was pretty sure Pan had put on weight since I first met him. I mean, he wasn't as well fed as his uncle, that was for sure, but it's not like he was wasting away, either.

Pan's relatives looked at each other with stunned expressions.

"Maria," said Uncle Fernando, "maybe I got some water in my ears back there ... or did that human just lecture us about the dietary habits of Mini-Dragons?"

"Thinks he knows all about us because he read it in some book," said Aunt Maria.

"Know better than us, do you, boy?" shouted Uncle Fernando, puffing out his chest.

"No, no..." I said, taking a step backwards and accidentally knocking over a bottle of shampoo and a Scuba Dave toy that had been resting on the end of the bath.

Aunt Maria peered at me over her sunglasses. "A bit old for toys, aren't we?" she said.

"I'm nine," I said defensively.

"Exactly," she replied.

My face flushed red as I put the bottle and the toy back. I tried to think of a clever reply, but all I could manage was, "Get lost."

"How dare you speak to my wife like that!" said Uncle Fernando, holding up his tiny claws as fists.

Aunt Maria touched her husband's arm.

"Leave it, Fernando, he's not worth it."

Uncle Fernando nodded. "You're right, my love," he said, dropping his arms. "Typical human. I just can't stand them."

Pan, Min, Jayden and I frowned in unison. "What's wrong with humans?" Min asked.

Aunt Maria put her head in her hands. "Oh no," she groaned. "You had to ask. Now he's going to do the song."

Uncle Fernando spread his wings, flew up and perched himself on the edge of the bath. "I'll tell you what's wrong with humans." He started to sing:

They're big and they're smelly,
With bellies like ... *gelatine*
They're mean and they're crude,
And incredibly... *impolite*.
They're foolish and cruel,
And they think they look... *fashionable*.
They destroy and they fight,
And always think they're... *correct*.
And that's what's wrong with HUUUUMANS!

There was an awkward silence as
Uncle Fernando took a bow before flying
back down. Aunt Maria gave him an
embarrassed clap.

"You know," said Min thoughtfully. "If you
changed a few of those words, you could
make it rhyme."

Uncle Fernando's face went bright red
with anger. "And they're obsessed with
rhymes!" he shouted. "If I wanted criticism,

I would have asked for it. Pan, get over here, we're leaving."

"Already?" I said.

The four of us looked at each other in horror.

"But you just got here!" said Jayden.

"Yes, and it's already been too long," said Aunt Maria, turning up her snout. She undid the straps on Uncle Fernando's backpack and removed a folded-up wetsuit and another small glass helmet. She tossed them to Pan. "Your uncle made you this diving helmet for going underwater. Not that we're expecting any gratitude from you. Go on, put it on."

"I'm not getting in the toilet," said Pan.

"Oh yes, you are, sunshine," said Uncle Fernando, as he and Aunt Maria started putting their wetsuits back on.

"Just be grateful that we're not making

you fly once we reach the ocean," said Aunt Maria. "Your poor uncle is going to have to carry you to Mexico. And him with his back."

Uncle Fernando flexed his flabby arms. "Lucky for you, Pan, I've still got these bad boys. You don't get this sort of strength from prawn crackers, trust me."

"You can't go yet!" I said.

Uncle Fernando placed his hands on his hips. "Oh? And why is that?"

It was a good question, and one I didn't have an answer for. My mind scrambled for a solution, but drew a blank. As everyone waited for me to speak, I glanced down at Pan, who gave me a wink before tossing the glass helmet into the air. It came as high as my chin before plummeting back to the ground.

SMASH!

All heads turned towards Pan, the helmet at his feet, smashed to pieces.

"Whoops," said Pan.

CHAPTER 7

GETTING TO KNOW YOU

"You did that on purpose!" shouted Uncle Fernando.

"No, I didn't," said Pan. "It just slipped." He was trying his best to look convincing, but I don't think anyone believed him.

"Can it be fixed?" asked Aunt Maria.

Uncle Fernando considered the shattered bits of glass on the floor, examining a couple of pieces in his hands. "Some careful fire breathing should do the trick. But it'll take some time. We'll need to stay the night."

Aunt Maria looked repulsed. "US?" she

cried. "Staying with HUMANS? Don't you remember your own song? Can't we go somewhere else and come back when it's fixed?"

"Yes!" said Pan. "That sounds like a great idea."

"I'm not exactly thrilled with the situation myself, Maria," said Uncle Fernando, ignoring Pan, "but that Mini-Dragon needs to be watched. You know he smashed that helmet on purpose. He has no respect – and who do you think he got that from?"

Aunt Maria gave Min, Jayden and me a dirty look.

"Exactly," said Uncle Fernando. "So I'm not leaving him unsupervised with the humans. We'll stay here tonight, I'll get the helmet fixed, then we'll leave first thing in the morning."

Aunt Maria folded her arms, pouting.

"Fine," she mumbled.

As happy as I was that Pan wasn't going anywhere, for the night at least, the thought of sharing my bedroom with another two Mini-Dragons didn't exactly fill me with joy.

I was running out of drawers for a start.

Uncle Fernando carefully placed the broken pieces into his backpack, then after hastily cleaning up the bathroom with a couple of towels, I managed to get everyone back into my room. It wasn't long before Pan's uncle had taken to my desk as if it were a stage. As he told us all about their trip from Mexico to Spain to England in excruciating detail, Min and Jayden conveniently remembered they had to go home. Aunt Maria sat on the end of the desk chair, filing her claws. She mostly ignored her husband but occasionally piped up when he got a bit of the story wrong. Pan and I, meanwhile, lay on my bed. Pan had already drifted off and I was beginning to feel my own eyes getting heavy when we heard a noise.

DIIIIIIIIING-DONGGGGG

"What's a 'ding-dong'?" asked Aunt Maria.

Pan let out a yawn before shaking his head. "That's the doorbell," he said. "It tells you that there's someone at the door."

"It'll be Toby round for his dinner," I said to Pan. "Can you keep an eye on them, make sure they don't do … well, anything really."

"I doubt it," sighed Pan, "but I'll try."

To give you an idea of how bad it was being in the company of Pan's aunt and uncle I had never been so happy to see Toby in all my life.

"Toby!" I said, greeting him at the front door. "It's great to see you."

"What? No, it isn't," said Toby, barging past me.

"Yes, it is," I said. "Come through, I think Mum's made hot dogs tonight."

Toby hung up his coat then grunted something that sounded like approval as we entered the kitchen.

"Mum, Dad, look who's here," I said cheerfully.

My parents looked at me, then each other. "Everything OK, Eric?" asked Dad.

"Fine, thanks," I said. "Just happy Toby's here, that's all."

Mum put her hand on my forehead.
"Hmm … he doesn't have a temperature,"
she said. "You sure you're not ill? Do you
want to go upstairs and have a lie-down?"

"No!" I blurted out. Going back upstairs
was the last thing I wanted to do. "Honestly,
I'm fine."

SNAP!

"Now, Posy, no camera at the table,"
said Mum, taking the device off her. Posy,
strapped into her high chair, reacted
exactly how you would expect a two-and-
a-half-year-old to react to having their
favourite toy taken away – she cried. A lot.

"Oh dear," said Dad. "She loves that
thing."

"Mum got me one of those," said Toby,
as he tucked into a hot dog – it'd take more
than a screaming toddler to distract Toby
from his food. "Bit more advanced than

Posy's obviously. It's top-of-the-range kit – just like the pros use. *Really* expensive."

For some reason, it quickly came back to me how annoying Toby was.

I normally hated playing video games with Toby. I always had to lose or else he'd find a way to get me in trouble. But tonight I was just glad I didn't have to go back upstairs for a while. Still, I couldn't help feeling guilty for leaving Pan to deal with his aunt and uncle by himself.

Once Toby had left it was time to face the music and I made my way up the stairs. But when I got to my room I found Pan by himself, reading comics and chomping away on some prawn crackers. In a period of just a few seconds I went through five distinct stages:

1. Relief — phew! They weren't here.

2. Hope — Maybe they'd changed their minds and gone home without Pan.

3. Doubt — That didn't seem likely...

4. Sadness — No, there was no chance that was what had happened.

5. Fear — So where were they and what were they up to?

"They've gone to find something to eat," said Pan. "I told them not to leave, but they wouldn't listen."

"How hard did you try?" I asked.

"Not very," admitted Pan. "In fact I ... er... Never mind."

I looked at Pan suspiciously. "What were you going to say?"

Pan put down the comic book. "All right... Well, I sort of had an idea for how to get rid of them."

I could tell this wasn't going to be good. "An idea?"

"Yeah," said Pan, nodding. "I offered them some prawn crackers, but they laughed in my face. They said they needed something with a bit of meat on it. So I told them where they could find food like that. Nearby."

I thought about this for a few moments. Then the penny dropped and I let out a huge gasp. "Not Pusskin?" I said.

"It's not as bad as it sounds," he said.

I thought about this. "Are you sure?

Because it sounds quite bad to me. You sent your aunt and uncle to eat my cat!"

"OK, when you put it like that it sounds bad," said Pan. "But don't worry, my aunt and uncle are terrible hunters. Pusskin's not in any trouble. I'm figuring she'll take one look at them and run them out of town."

"And if she doesn't?" I asked, not entirely sure who I was more worried about – Pusskin or the Mini-Dragons.

"Haven't really thought that far," admitted Pan.

"ARRRRRRRRGHHHHH!" screamed a voice that was unmistakably Pan's aunt.

Pan and I looked at each other in horror, then bolted out of the door.

"Eric, is everything all right?" shouted Mum from downstairs.

"Fine, Mum," I shouted back. "I just … stubbed my toe on my bed."

"Ouch. OK, well, be careful."

In actual fact, the scream had come from Posy's bedroom. We opened the door to find a petrified Aunt Maria trembling in one corner of the room, and Pusskin in the other.

"Where's Uncle Fernando?" I asked.

"I think that's his legs, there," said Pan. "Hanging out of Pusskin's mouth."

CHAPTER 8

THE MEXICAN STAND-OFF

It's difficult to know what to do in situations like these. Situations where your friend's uncle is being eaten by your cat.

Do you:

a) Demand the cat release the uncle (which could backfire — cats are not reasonable creatures and don't like to negotiate).

b) Wrestle the cat to the ground and extract the uncle from its jaws (this will almost surely result in you walking away with a million scratches — if you walk away at all, that is).

I had to admit c) did have a certain appeal. If Uncle Fernando escaped then great, I guess. But if he didn't then ... Pan would have to stay! No way could Aunt Maria carry him back to Mexico. Wait – how on earth could I think that? What kind of monster was I?

"Help him!" screamed Aunt Maria.

I made a move towards Pusskin, but Pan shot ahead of me until he was about a metre away from the greedy feline.

"Pusskin," he said in a low voice. "I want you to release my uncle. We can do this the easy way or the hard way."

Pusskin stared at Pan, unblinking. Uncle Fernando's legs wriggled helplessly, which at least confirmed he was still alive. Just

98

when it looked like Pusskin wasn't going
to back down, Pan took a deep intake of
breath and released a huge burst of flame
that came within centimetres of the cat's face
– and Uncle Fernando's legs.

Now, Pusskin didn't like a lot of things
including, but not limited to:

- People
- Cheap cat food
- Anyone sitting on her favourite spot on the couch
- Dogs
- Other cats
- The vet (see, people)
- Baths
- Brushes
- Being fried to a crisp by Mini-Dragons

Of all the things Pusskin hates, that
last one is probably the most important

one here. She spat out Uncle Fernando, sending him skidding across the room in a trail of saliva, before bolting out of the room, almost knocking over Posy who was standing in the hall. Seeing her, I quickly closed the door and made a mental note to check her camera later.

"Fernando!" wailed Aunt Maria, flinging herself into his arms, only to realize that she too was now covered in cat saliva. **"Eeeeuuuuurrrrrghhhhh!"** she cried, shoving him away.

"Just so everyone's clear," I said, looking directly at Pan, who was avoiding my gaze. "There will be no more hunting of my cat."

"Maybe if you'd put on a decent spread for your guests, instead of prawn crackers, they wouldn't have been forced to find their own food," said Aunt Maria.

"It looked to me like the only one finding

food was Pusskin," I said. "It wouldn't kill you to thank Pan, by the way. He did just save your life."

"He's the one who told us where to find the cat," said Uncle Fernando. "He didn't say anything about it being a ruthless killing machine. Although obviously I had the situation under control. Two more seconds and I would have toasted the big furball."

I rolled my eyes.

"Come on, Uncle Fernando," sighed Pan. "Let's get you cleaned up."

"That's the first sensible thing you've said since we got here," he replied.

Pan led his relatives through to the bathroom. When we got there, Pan and I watched them with curiosity. They weren't heading towards the sink. They weren't even heading towards the bath or the shower.

I looked at Pan. "They're not...?" I said.

They were.
PLONK!
PLONK!
They were in the toilet. *Again.*

"Ah, the water's lovely," said Uncle
Fernando.

"It's the only decent thing in this place,"
agreed Aunt Maria.

"I thought dragons hated water?" I said, remembering a note from the *Encyclopaedia Dragonica*.

"We're washing ourselves," came Uncle Fernando's voice from the toilet bowl. "Not drinking it – that would be disgusting."

"Yeah, *that* would be disgusting," said Pan sarcastically.

I frowned. There was water all over the floor. "I just cleaned this place," I sighed, grabbing another towel.

"Bit of manual labour never hurt anyone," said Uncle Fernando. "They'll be plenty of that waiting for you back in Mexico, Pan. We'll build some character in you yet, mark my words."

A gloomy-looking Pan slumped to the floor. It was going to be horrible not having Pan around, but I realized that it would be much worse for him having to live with those two. I wished I could just make our problems disappear.

Then I realized I could. My eyes had drifted to the toilet handle.

It would be so easy.

I could literally flush our problems away. So easy...

No, I thought. It wouldn't work. True enough, they didn't have their wetsuits, but I had no doubt they'd still manage to get back somehow.

Still ... we might get a couple of hours without them, which would be nice.

No, it was a crazy idea. There's no way I could do it.

"Hey, how about a bit of soap down here?" shouted Uncle Fernando.

FLUSH!!!

I stood there for a few moments in stunned silence. Slowly I turned my head

towards the toilet handle where Pan now
dangled from it, a look of regret on his face.

"I'm sorry," he said. "Did you want to do
that?"

When Pan's aunt and uncle eventually showed up again, they were not happy.

Obviously.

My bedroom door opened and the two of them stepped in, soaked from head to tail, and fuming. Pan and I tried our best not to laugh, but it was tough.

"You flushed us down the toilet!" said Aunt Maria, pointing a claw at Pan.

"While we were bathing, I might add," said Uncle Fernando, as if that somehow made it worse.

"Did he put you up to it?" asked Aunt Maria, pointing towards me.

"No," snapped Pan. "I did it myself, because I don't want you here. And I don't want to live with you. I want to stay with Eric."

"Mini-Dragons don't belong with

humans!" shouted Uncle Fernando. "You're coming home with us and that's the end of it." He snatched the facecloth I had offered them. After drying himself, he took a bite out of the material.

Aunt Maria looked appalled. "Fernando! Junk food!"

"I'm starving, Maria!" he said. "I haven't had a goat in days and in the last few hours I've been nearly eaten by a cat and flushed down the toilet. Would you rather I ate a prawn cracker?"

For the rest of the night, the atmosphere in my room was tense to say the least. Uncle Fernando worked alone on the top of my chest of drawers, repairing the broken helmet by fusing the pieces back together with his dragon breath. Pan sulked in his sock drawer. I pretended I had some homework to do, and Aunt Maria went to bed early.

My bed.

Uncle Fernando and Aunt Maria refused to sleep in my drawers and, with the mood they were in, I didn't feel like arguing with them.

So at bedtime I took a spare blanket and pillow out of the cupboard, lay down on the floor and fell asleep.

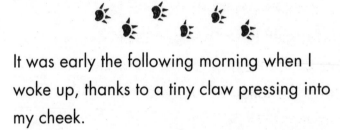

It was early the following morning when I woke up, thanks to a tiny claw pressing into my cheek.

"Pan?" I yawned. "What do you want?"

"Shhh!" he whispered. He pointed towards my bed, where I could hear the sound of two Mini-Dragons snoring. "I think I have a plan to get rid of them for good."

I rubbed my eyes, still half asleep. "Pan, you've already tried feeding them to my cat and flushing them down the toilet. What else can you possibly come up with?"

Pan whispered in my ear.

I sat bolt upright, completely awake.

I didn't think it was possible, but Pan had come up with an idea that made the others seem harmless.

It was terrifying.

It was crossing a line.

It might just work.

CHAPTER 9

AN UNEXPECTED GIFT

Toby's mum answered the door wearing a
fluffy pink dressing gown, her normally neat
hair looking like a lion's mane, shooting off
in all directions. But some things
never change – she was still
tapping away on her phone,
barely acknowledging me.

"Is Toby there?" I asked.

Her eyes drifted briefly
from the screen to me then
back again. She walked
off without saying a word.

Moments later a bleary-eyed Toby appeared wearing what I knew was a very expensive pair of silk pyjamas. I knew because, like with all his things, he made sure I knew what they cost.

"Crispo?" he said. "Do you know what time it is?"

"Sorry, I know it's early," I said.

"What do you want?" yawned Toby.

"Here," I said, shoving a taped-up shoebox into his hands.

"What's this?" he asked.

"It's something you've wanted for ages," I said.

Toby's eyes lit up. "A Ferrari?"

"What? No!" I said, shaking my head. "How would I even... No – the *other* thing you've wanted for ages."

Toby had to think for a moment or two. "You don't mean...? Not the dragon toy?"

I nodded. "Yes. Well, no, not that one. But one just like it. Two, in fact."

Toby suddenly didn't seem so tired any more. In fact, I couldn't remember seeing him more alert. "*Two* dragon toys?" he said. "Just like that?"

"Just like that," I said.

Toby went to open the box, but I put my hand on his. "No," I said firmly. "Not here. Wait until you're inside."

Toby looked at me suspiciously. "What's going on? Why would you give these to me? Where did you even get them? I can't find them anywhere."

"Enough questions," I said. "Do you want them or not?"

Toby looked at the box. "Well, yeah, of course, but—"

"Great," I said. "Enjoy!"

I turned and ran back towards my

house, leaving before Toby could utter another word.

Pan and I sat on the end of my bed, contemplating what we had just done.

"Min and Jayden are coming around this morning," I said, trying to break the silence.

"Oh?" said Pan quietly. "That'll be nice. Do you think we should have told my aunt and uncle that Toby thinks we're all toys? To avoid confusion, I mean?"

I thought about this, then shook my head. "No," I said. "We would have had to wake them up first for that. And they wouldn't have listened anyway."

Pan nodded and we returned to sitting in silence.

"We're horrible, aren't we?" I said,

after a while.

Pan nodded. "A little bit," he said. "Not as horrible as they are."

"But we just gave your horrible aunt and uncle to the most horrible person we know. That makes us horrible times horrible."

"We're horrible squared?" asked Pan.

"I think so," I said.

A picture formed in my head of Toby playing with the Mini-Dragons. What if he wanted them to light their own farts like he had seen Pan do once? Somehow I couldn't picture Aunt Maria agreeing to that. But Toby doesn't like to take no for an answer. I imagined him tearing the two of them apart, looking for the buttons that made them breathe fire.

I knew what we had to do.

"We have to get them back," I said, with zero enthusiasm.

Pan let out a resigned groan. "You're right. We can't just leave them with Toby. No one deserves that."

It was going to be easier said than done though. Toby had wanted a Mini-Dragon 'toy' for ages – he wasn't going to hand them over without a fight.

There was a knock at the door. Pan and I looked at each other.

A few moments later, Dad shouted up the stairs. "Eric, that's Toby at the door for you."

Downstairs, I found a very agitated and jittery Toby waiting for me. Before I could open my mouth, he had shoved the shoebox back into my hands.

Then he ran away.

"Well, that can't be good," I said to myself. I hated to imagine what could have happened for Toby to give them up so easily.

I brought the box back up to my room
then opened the lid. Two very angry Mini-
Dragons glared back at me.

"Oh, there you are!" I said, hoping to
sound relieved that we had found them.

"Don't either of you even try to talk your

way out of this one," said Uncle Fernando, as they both flew out of the box and perched themselves on my chest of drawers.

"What did you do to Toby?" I asked.

"Toby?" said Uncle Fernando. "Is that what you call him? The silly boy seemed to think we were toys. Kept putting us up on his shelf. So I tried giving him a history lesson on Mini-Dragons, but then he started yammering on about finding my 'Off' switch until eventually he bundles us back into the box. A very rude young man, but no more than I've come to expect from humans."

"You're in for it now," said Aunt Maria, shaking a claw at Pan.

Pan didn't seem to care. "Oh yeah? It's not like you could do anything worse to me than make me go and live with you."

"I wouldn't be so sure about that," said Uncle Fernando. "There's still one thing we can do that you'll dislike even more."

"And what's that?" asked Pan, folding his arms.

Aunt Maria gave her nephew a cruel smirk, before saying, "We're going to tell your mum on you!"

CHAPTER 10
FAMILY REUNION

"Eric, your friends are here," shouted Mum.

"Thanks, Mum," I said, rushing down the stairs to greet Min and Jayden. "Can we keep using the computer?"

"OK," she replied. "But remember I'll need it in a little while for my class."

At the top of the stairs, Min and Jayden looked at me with concern. "Everything all right, Eric?" asked Jayden.

"No," I said, before filling them in on our attempts to get rid of the unwelcome Mini-Dragons.

"Wow," said Min. "You really handed them over to Toby?"

I nodded. "Although it's probably Toby we should feel sorry for."

"Where are they now?" asked Jayden.

"They're in the computer room speaking to Pan's parents," I said. "Getting him into trouble. But I have an idea."

Min frowned. "It doesn't sound like your ideas have been that great recently."

"I know," I said. "But this is our last shot. The helmet's fixed so Fernando and Maria want to take Pan away this morning. We have to convince Pan's parents to let him stay."

The three Mini-Dragons were gathered around the laptop screen, furiously shouting over the top of each other, as Pan's parents looked on with weary expressions. It was impossible to make out what anyone was

saying, especially since they were all talking
in their dragon language.

"QUIET!" Pan's mum shouted at last, silencing the room. I guessed from the way she was looking at us that the switch to English was for our benefit. Whatever she had to say, she wanted everyone to hear it. She reminded me of my own mum in a lot of ways. She was kind-hearted, but there was definitely a side of her that you didn't want to mess with.

"Pan," she said in a much lower voice, "I'm very disappointed with you. Your behaviour is unacceptable. First you smash your diving helmet, which I don't believe for a second was an accident. Then you send your uncle off to hunt a cat ... when you know perfectly well your uncle is a hopeless hunter."

"Hey!" protested Uncle Fernando.

"Then you flush them down the toilet," continued Mrs Long, ignoring Fernando.

"And *then* you bundle them into a box and give them away!"

"We didn't raise you to behave like that, did we?" said Pan's dad.

Pan shook his head.

"He'd better not behave like this when he's living with us," said Aunt Maria.

"I don't want to live with you!" shouted Pan.

"Now, son," said Pan's dad, "we've been over this. Until it's safe for you to return to China, you have to live with your aunt and uncle. Only other Mini-Dragons can teach you the ancient Mini-Dragon ways."

Pan didn't look convinced. "Ancient Mini-Dragon ways?" he said. "Like the dragon codes that only dragons know how to use?"

"Exactly," said Pan's dad.

"That Eric managed to figure out in, like, five seconds?" said Pan.

His father squirmed a little. "Well … all right, so he got lucky there. But only a Mini-Dragon can bestow upon another Mini-Dragon the five qualities they must have if they're to become well-rounded adults. Leadership, Ingenuity, Bravery, Loyalty and Kindness.

Pan's aunt and uncle nodded smugly in agreement, not that I had seen them display any of those qualities themselves.

"But Pan already has all of these things," I said.

"Oh yes," said Aunt Maria, smirking. "He was very kind when he flushed us down the toilet. And *so* loyal when he gave us away. How brave he was sending us off to get eaten! What ingenuity he showed when smashing his helmet! And he displays such tremendous leadership letting himself be brainwashed by a human!"

The room fell silent. Everyone was looking at me for a response. I could feel my blood boiling. There had to be a way to prove them wrong.

"I'll be right back," I said, rushing out of the door.

I found Posy downstairs looking at a book with Dad. She caught sight of me, smiled then raised her little camera and almost blinded me with the flash.

"Thought I'd take Posy through some of the photo albums," said Dad. "As it looks like we've got a little photographer on our hands here."

"Hey, Posy," I said. "Would it be OK if I borrowed your camera for a bit?"

"Oh-kay," she said, handing it to me.

Out of curiosity, I picked up the photo album and quickly thumbed through it. "Actually, can I borrow this, too?" I asked.

"Sure," said Dad, giving me an odd look. "What for, exactly?"

"Just a little project I'm working on," I shouted, as I raced up the stairs.

CHAPTER 11
THE CASE FOR PAN TO STAY

I burst into the room, put down the photo album and started scrolling through the hundreds of pictures Posy had taken on the camera. As I neared the end, I almost fell over. What I had been looking for was there, but there was also something even better.

"Eric, is everything all right?" asked Pan.

"The boy's completely lost it," muttered Uncle Fernando.

"No, I haven't," I said, "and everything's fine. Better than fine." I plugged the camera into the laptop and started clicking away.

"OK," I said at last, looking directly at Pan's parents on the screen. "You want leadership? Take a look at this."

I attached the files and clicked the send button on the computer. It made a little whooshing noise as it sent a bunch of images to Pan's parents. I watched as they opened the email on screen.

"I don't understand," said Pan's mum. "What am I looking at?"

I double-clicked on the files so that everyone could see the pictures. Images of a party in full flow appeared on the screen. "These," I said, "are photographs taken from my parents' surprise party. A party that Pan organized every last detail of – from the invites to the decorations to the music to the colour of the balloons. He arranged it all. How's that for leadership?"

Pan's parents looked impressed. "You did all that?" asked his father.

Pan nodded.

"That woman in the photos reminds me of someone," said Mrs Long, before shaking her head. "Well, I mean, it's very impressive but still—"

"I'm not finished," I interrupted. "There's more. I'm sending you a video file."

I couldn't believe it was on there. Posy had been hanging around outside the room when it happened, she must have been filming at the same time. I opened the file. The footage was pretty shaky – probably about as good as you could expect from a two-and-a-half-year-old who had accidentally switched the camera on to video mode – but it was good enough to show the moment when Pan confronted Pusskin and saved his uncle's life.

Pan's parents let out huge gasps.

"My little boy!" said his mum, holding her claws over her mouth. "So brave!"

"Good job, son!" said his dad, beaming with pride.

An indignant Uncle Fernando sniffed. "I had a perfectly good plan for escaping," he said.

"Was your plan to let Pusskin choke on you?" asked Jayden, causing everyone to burst out laughing. Except Pan's aunt and uncle, of course.

Min must have figured out what I was trying to do, as she was already flicking through the photo album. Her face lit up as she removed a photo and held it up to the screen. It was a picture of my dad and the football team he managed, the Kippers, celebrating on the pitch.

"Here's loyalty," she said, her face beaming with pride. "This is a picture of Eric's dad's football team after winning their second game in history – thanks to Pan, who stayed up all night working on their tactics after he accidentally set them on fire and got Eric into heaps of trouble."

There was a brief silence as it seemed to dawn on Min that the last part of that story didn't make Pan sound so good.

"Moving on," said Jayden quickly, who was also holding a photo. He held it up to the screen. It was a picture taken from my ninth birthday party, with Toby shooting through the air on my electric scooter. "Ingenuity," said Jayden. "Pan once made a scooter fly."

Of course Jayden had left out the part about Pan doing this by accident. And the part where the scooter crashed into a tree moments later.

Pan's dad had an excited look on his face. "I had no idea you were into tinkering," he said, looking admiringly at Pan. "Chip off the old claw, eh? Have you done anything else?"

"Well, I once made a golf cart go faster than a car," admitted Pan.

"Wow!" said his father. "That's

amazing. You must tell me all about it sometime."

"I will," said a grinning Pan.

It looked like we were starting to win over Mr Long, but I wasn't so sure about his wife. She looked delighted to hear good things about her son, but she had that same pained look on her face that my mum got when it was time to break it to me that I had to go to the dentist.

So I looked directly at her.

"Pan is the kindest person or Mini-Dragon I know, Mrs Long," I said. "These things he's done, they were all to help others. You don't have to worry about him learning those Mini-Dragon qualities. He already has them."

Everyone was looking at me in amazement. There was complete silence.

"I've never heard such rubbish in all my life," said Aunt Maria.

"Oh, put a sock in it, Maria," said Pan's dad. "Can't you see what's happened here?"

If she did then she was too outraged to say.

"At some point in their life, every Mini-Dragon will seek out a companion," said Mr Long in a solemn voice. "The bond that forms between them will last a lifetime. Of course, the companion is almost always another Mini-Dragon, but it has been known for it to be a human. It happened to my own brother, actually. He became friends with a man – a mountain climber who stumbled across his cave one day. They ended up writing a book together, all about dragons. It was called—"

"*The Encyclopaedia Dragonica*?" interrupted Min.

"Oh, you've heard of it!" said Pan's dad, looking impressed. "Anyway, a Mini-Dragon companionship is not something that should be broken lightly." He turned to his wife. "I think perhaps we should reconsider…"

I was ready to start celebrating there and then, until I saw Mrs Long's face.

"I'm sorry," she said, shaking her head. "Everything you've told me is wonderful, Eric. Pan, I'm so proud of you. And I'm very happy that you've met these wonderful people. But a Mini-Dragon's place is with other Mini-Dragons. I won't change my mind on the subject."

"But Mum—" protested Pan.

He was cut off by the sound of the door opening.

"All right, Eric, that's time," said Mum, standing in the doorway, decked out in her yoga gear.

Everyone froze. The Mini-Dragons had *actually* frozen, but Min, Jayden and I were glued to the spot as well. In fact, as Mum looked around the room, it felt like time itself had stopped.

Eventually, she let out a little chuckle. "What is it with you kids and dragons at the moment?" she said. She looked at Min and Jayden while pointing towards Aunt Maria and Uncle Fernando. "I presume those two are yours?"

Min and Jayden nodded slowly.

"And that'll be the video game, no doubt," she said, pointing towards the laptop where Mr and Mrs Long stared, motionless, from the screen. "Anyway, wrap things up, Eric, I'll be starting my class soon."

"Yes, Mum," I said, my voice barely a whisper.

When the door closed behind us, I almost fell over in relief.

"That was close," said Jayden.

"Pan can stay," a voice murmured.

"Yeah, I know," I said to Jayden.

"I thought Mum was definitely about to…
Wait, what was that?"

All heads turned towards the screen.

"Pan can stay," repeated Mrs Long.

"He can?" said her husband, looking as
shocked as everyone else.

"Don't you know who that was?" she said,
as she fanned her face with her tiny claws.
"That was the yoga woman! Pan's staying
with the yoga woman!"

"The one from the internet?" asked Pan's
dad.

Mrs Long nodded, giddy with excitement. "My son is staying with the famous yoga lady. Wait till I tell all my friends!" She looked at me. "Can you get her autograph for me, Eric?"

"No problem," I laughed.

I couldn't believe it. Pan was staying. I had never felt so happy in all my life.
I looked around to find him.

He wasn't there.

Neither were his aunt and uncle.

CHAPTER 12
DOWN THE PAN

"Hold it right there!" I said, bursting into the bathroom. Instinctively, I knew that's where they would be. Pan's aunt and uncle were perched on the edge of the toilet with Pan trapped underneath Uncle Fernando's right arm. He was wriggling furiously, trying to escape, but his uncle was far too strong for him. The three of them were already dressed in their wetsuits. Aunt Maria slammed the glass helmet on to Pan's head.

"Adios, humans," said Uncle Fernando, giving us all a farewell salute.

"Don't you dare!" shouted Pan's mum, as Jayden and Min arrived behind me, Jayden carrying the laptop in his arms.

"Honestly, Isabel, you're not thinking straight," said Aunt Maria. "Letting your son stay with a human? It's preposterous! No, you'll come to thank us for this, trust me. It's for the best."

"Leave him, Maria," demanded Pan's dad. "Or so help me, we'll come and get him from you ourselves."

Uncle Fernando let out a dismissive chuckle. "Good luck with that, Cheng," he said. "Mexico is nearly two-million-square kilometres and we don't stay in the same spot for very long. Actually, maybe we won't even go back to Mexico. Wherever we go, you'll never find us. We'll be sure to send you a postcard from time to time though."

A desperate Pan managed to wriggle his arms free and flung the helmet to the floor, smashing it to pieces once again. Min, Jayden and I let out a cheer, but our celebration was short-lived.

"Thought you might try that," said Aunt Maria. "You can wear this instead." She strapped a tiny scuba mask on Pan's head –

it was the one from my Scuba Dave bath toy.

"Don't worry about Pan," laughed Uncle Fernando. "He'll be much better off with us. Now, as the British like to say: Cheerio!"

And with that, Aunt Maria and Uncle Fernando dived into the toilet, dragging Pan along behind them.

"Pan!" cried Min.

"No!" shouted Jayden.

"My boy!" gasped Pan's dad.

I turned towards the screen. Pan's mum had a steely look in her eyes.

"Do something," she said.

It wasn't a plea. It was an order. And once again, I got the distinct impression that when Mrs Long told you to do something, you did it.

She really was a lot like my own mum.

I ran over to the toilet, unsure what my next move was going to be. I thought about

146

jumping in after them but decided against it because it was:

a) Disgusting

b) Pointless, since I wouldn't fit

c) Disgusting

Then I saw the plunger.

I grabbed the handle, shoved it into the toilet bowl and began pumping as if my life depended on it. Then, after about a minute...

...nothing happened.

I kept going.

"Eric," said Min after a while, laying a hand on my shoulder. "I think they've gone."

"No," I said. If I stopped I knew I'd definitely never see Pan again.

"Come on, mate," said Jayden. "You've done all you can."

"No," I repeated.

"It's OK, Eric," said Pan's dad quietly. "You gave it your best shot. Pan's lucky to have a friend like you."

"I'm. Not. Stopping." I said. "Not. Now. Not. Ev—"

Before I could finish I was sent flying backwards as a stream of water shot out of the toilet, followed by the sound of one … two … three solid objects splashing back into the toilet.

"Pan!" I cried, throwing aside the plunger and fishing him out.

"Eric!" said Pan, tossing his mask back into the toilet bowl. "You saved me."

"What are you thinking!" shouted a livid Uncle Fernando.

"You're making a big mistake," screamed Aunt Maria.

"The only mistake," said Pan's mum, "was thinking it was a good idea for you two to look after our son. I think it's time you were on your way."

"Here, let me get the door for you," I added, reaching for the toilet handle.

FLUSH!!!

I looked at Pan, perched on my shoulder, still dripping wet, his mouth hanging wide open.

"I'm sorry," I said. "Did you want to do that?"

A couple of days later and things were back to normal. Well, as normal as life with a Mini-Dragon can ever be. Which is not very normal. It was great to have Pan back and know that he wasn't going anywhere. It was even better to have Pan's aunt and uncle gone.

Min, Jayden, Pan and I had arranged to meet up later that morning, but before that I had an appointment to keep. Mr and Mrs Long had asked to speak to me. Alone.

"Hi, Eric," said Pan's dad. "We just want to thank you again."

"No problem, Mr Long," I said. "I'd do anything for Pan."

Pan's parents smiled. "We're glad to hear you say that," said his mother.

"Oh? Why's that?" I asked.

"Well," she said, "since Pan won't be staying with his aunt and uncle, there's the matter of his education to address."

I shifted a little uncomfortably. "You mean Pan ... in school?" I said nervously. "We sort of tried that once before and it didn't end very well..."

"No," said Pan's dad, "not school. But there are certain things a dragon must learn."

"And as Pan's companion," continued his mum. "It's *your* job to make sure he learns them."

"It is?" I asked.

"*It is*," said Pan's parents firmly.

"Don't look so worried," said Pan's dad. "There's not a lot to it. I'm emailing you a file with all the information you'll need. It's only ten thousand words or so."

I nearly fell off my chair.

"T-t-ten thousand words?" I stammered.

"Or so," said Mr Long.

"Well, I suppose we'd better leave you to it then," said Pan's mum. "No time like the present!"

Hang on – they wanted me to start now?

"It's the school holidays!" I said.

"Wonderful!" said Mrs Long. "So you'll have plenty of free time to devote to Pan's studies. We'll be expecting regular updates on his progress. Anyway, we'll be off now. Oh, any word on that other thing I asked you about?"

I frowned. "Yes, I've posted you the autograph," I sighed, cringing at the memory of having to ask Mum for it, telling her it was for me – she thought I'd gone mad.

I said goodbye to Pan's parents, then opened up the file they had sent. The list of tasks was endless. The first page alone said:

- Learn a dozen languages
- Invent your own language
- Read (and perform) all of Shakespeare's plays
- See the world
- Master the art of flame-cooking
- Learn to fly

I did a double-take when I read the last one. Pan had once shown me how good a flyer he is shortly after we had met. He flew like a rock, trashing my room in the process. The list of things I'd rather do than teach Pan how to fly included:

- Teach Toby how to share
- Teach Mum how to sing
- Teach Pusskin not to be evil
- Teach Dad how to successfully
- Manage a football team

Even flushing my head down the toilet sounded better.

In fact...

"You finished?" said Pan as I walked past my room. "What did my parents want? Hey, where are you going?"

I didn't reply as I walked into the bathroom.

"Eric?" said Pan, sounding concerned. "Eric? ERIC?"

FLUSH!!!

| SEND | SAVE | DISCARD |

FROM: Eric Crisp

TO: THELONGS_83@DRAGONNET.CN

SUBJECT: Thank you!

TRANSLATED FROM DRAGON

Hi Mum and Dad

Just a quick note to say thanks for letting me stay with Eric. He's such a great friend. And so funny! He's always coming up with hilarious jokes. Earlier, he had this good one. He said - wait till you hear this - that you guys had given him homework for me to do! LOL! Told you he was a laugh!

Actually, it was a joke wasn't

ABOUT THE AUTHOR

Tom Nicoll has been writing since he was at school, where he enjoyed trying to fit in as much silliness to his essays as he could possibly get away with. When not writing, he enjoys playing video games (especially the ones where he gets beaten by kids half his age from all over the world). He is also a big comedy, TV and movie nerd. Tom lives just outside Edinburgh with his wife, daughter and a cat that thinks it's a dog.

THERE'S A DRAGON IN MY TOILET!
is his third book for children.

ABOUT THE ILLUSTRATOR

Sarah Horne grew up in Derbyshire and spent much
of her childhood scampering in the nearby fields with
a few goats. Then she decided to be sensible and
studied Illustration at Falmouth College of Arts and
gained a Master's degree at Kingston University.

She now lives in London and
specializes in funny, inky illustration.

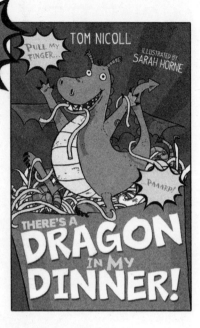

Find out more about
how Pan came to
live with Eric in...

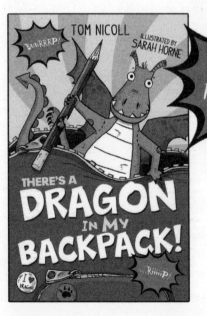

Eric agrees to take Pan
to school with him –
and quickly regrets it!